The Glaciers are Melting!

by Donna Love

illustrated by Shennen Bersani

Once upon a time, on a far away mountain, lived a little pika named Peter. As he stuck his head out of his rock doorway one day, a drop of water fell, **b-loop**, on his head.

"Great glaciers!" whistled Peter Pika. "The glaciers are melting . . . *the glaciers are melting?* If the glaciers melt, where will I live? I must go and ask the Mountain Monarch. He'll know what to do."

Peter Pika scrambled up the face of the mountain as fast as he could. On a high ledge, he met Tammy Ptarmigan.

"Where are you going?" Tammy Ptarmigan asked Peter Pika.

"The glaciers are melting," whistled Peter Pika. "And I'm going to tell the Mountain Monarch."

"Gleaming glaciers!" chirped Tammy Ptarmigan. "If the glaciers melt, will I still turn white in winter? I will go with you to ask the Mountain Monarch."

The two climbed onward until they came to Sally Squirrel.

"Where are you going?" Sally Squirrel asked Tammy Ptarmigan and Peter Pika.

"The glaciers are melting!" chirped Tammy Ptarmigan. "Peter Pika told me."

"Yes, a drop of it dripped on my head," whistled Peter Pika. "And we are going to tell the Mountain Monarch."

"Glistening glaciers!" squeaked Sally Squirrel. "If the glaciers melt, where will I sleep in winter? I will go with you to ask the Mountain Monarch."

The three climbed on until they met Mandy Marmot.

"Where are you going?" Mandy Marmot asked Sally Squirrel, Tammy Ptarmigan, and Peter Pika.

"The glaciers are melting!" squeaked Sally Squirrel.

"Peter Pika told us," chirped Tammy Ptarmigan.

"Yes, a drop of it dripped on my head," whistled Peter Pika. "And we are going to tell the Mountain Monarch."

"Glorious glaciers!" piped Mandy Marmot. "If the glaciers melt, will it be too hot in summer for all this fur? I will go with you to ask the Mountain Monarch."

The four climbers clambered on until they met Harry Hare.

"Where are you going?" Harry Hare asked Mandy Marmot, Sally Squirrel, Tammy Ptarmigan, and Peter Pika.

"The glaciers are melting," piped Mandy Marmot.

"Tammy Ptarmigan told me," squeaked Sally Squirrel.

"Peter Pika told me," chirped Tammy Ptarmigan.

"Yes, a drop of it dripped on my head," whistled Peter Pika. "And we are going to tell the Mountain Monarch."

"Golden glaciers!" squealed Harry Hare. "If the glaciers melt, how will I hop on the snow? I will go with you to ask the Mountain Monarch."

The five fine friends set out to climb the rest of the way up the mountain. Soon they grew tired and sat down to rest.

While they rested, Wiley Wolverine crept out from behind some rocks.

"Where are you going, my five fine friends?" hissed Wiley Wolverine with a sly grin.

"The glaciers are melting," squealed Harry Hare.

"Sally Squirrel told me," piped Mandy Marmot.

"Tammy Ptarmigan told me," squeaked Sally Squirrel.

"And Peter Pika told me," chirped Tammy Ptarmigan.

"Yes, a drop of it dripped on my head," whistled Peter Pika. "And we are going to tell the Mountain Monarch."

"**Ahh,** but you're not going the right way," hissed Wiley Wolverine. "The Mountain Monarch lives over here. Shall I show you the way?"

"Of course," said the five fine friends, and they followed Wiley Wolverine to the door of his den.

"This is a shortcut to the Mountain Monarch," hissed Wiley Wolverine.

The five fine friends looked at each other and asked, "Are you sure this is the way?"

"Of course it is," stated Wiley Wolverine, looking very sure of himself.

Just then, the Mountain Monarch jumped down from the rocks and said, "Don't go in there! It is Wiley Wolverine's home."

Then the Mountain Monarch butted Wiley Wolverine down the rocky mountainside. When Wiley Wolverine stopped tumbling, he got up and ran away.

"Now, tell me, my five fine friends," asked the Mountain Monarch. "What's all this I hear about the glaciers melting?"

Happy to escape, Harry Hare, Mandy Marmot, Sally Squirrel, Tammy Ptarmigan, and Peter Pika all started talking at once.

"The glaciers are melting," squealed Harry Hare.

"Sally Squirrel told me," piped Mandy Marmot.

"Tammy Ptarmigan told me," squeaked Sally Squirrel.

"And Peter Pika told me," chirped Tammy Ptarmigan.

"Yes, a drop of it dripped on my head," whistled Peter Pika. "So we came to ask you what to do."

The Mountain Monarch looked across the mountains.

"I was afraid of this," he said. "From my view high on the mountain, I see that the glaciers really are melting. Each year they get smaller and smaller."

The five fine friends asked, "What can we do?"

The Mountain Monarch looked sad and shook his head. Finally he said, "There are too few of us, so there is nothing we can do."

So Peter Pika asked, "Then who?"

For Creative Minds

Glaciers

If it snows where you live, it probably melts during the summer. But the North and South Poles and some mountain peaks have snow all year long. By mid to late summer, you can see a line (firn line) where the glacial ice and snow meet. Below the line, the snow melts. Above the line, the snow piles (accumulates) on top of the snow from earlier years. The weight of all the new snow turns the older snow into ice—like a metamorphic rock changed by pressure. When the ice gets as thick as 60 feet (about 18 meters) give or take, it becomes a glacier. It takes years for glaciers to form.

A "river of ice?" Rivers do not freeze to make glaciers, but glaciers do move. As the ice builds and the glacier gets heavier, gravity pulls it down.

Moving glaciers pick up rocks and dirt, carrying them along with the ice. The rocks and glaciers carve valleys, eroding the land as they move.

Some glaciers move slowly and others move quickly. You might hear loud noises from a fast-moving glacier.

During ancient ice ages and glaciations, some huge rocks were moved hundreds of miles. They are not like any rocks around them and are called "glacial eratics" or "out-of-place rocks."

Ice sheets or continental glaciers move out from their edges on flat land. Alpine glaciers are on mountains and flow down.

When glaciers melt, they "drop" the rocks and dirt, making new land called moraine.

Glaciers grow if snow collects year after year.
Glaciers stay the same size if ice melts at the same rate as the snow collects.
Glaciers shrink if the ice melts faster than the snow collects.

Are Glaciers Melting?

Compare the pictures of glaciers below.
Do you think the glaciers are growing, staying the same, or melting?

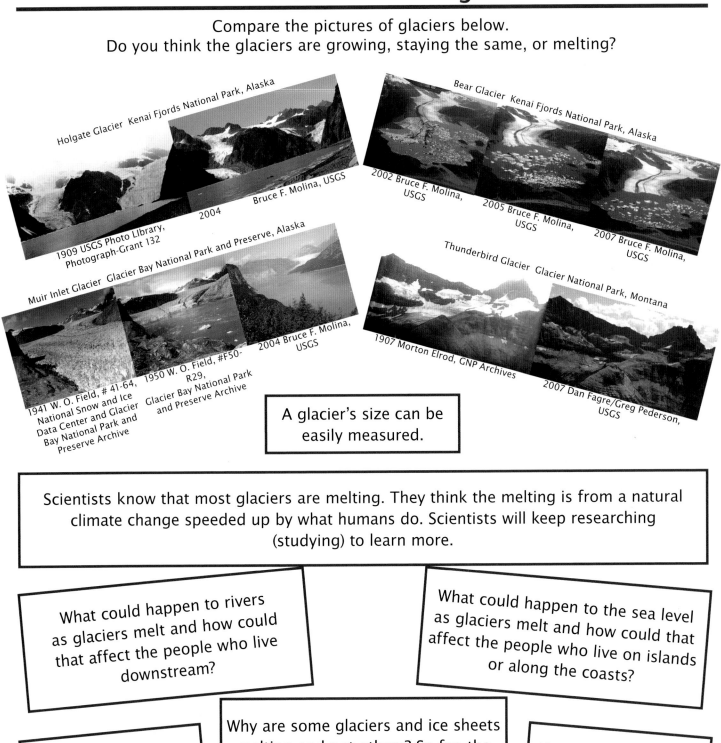

Holgate Glacier Kenai Fjords National Park, Alaska

Bruce F. Molina, USGS

2004

1909 USGS Photo Library, Photograph-Grant 132

Bear Glacier Kenai Fjords National Park, Alaska

2002 Bruce F. Molina, USGS

2005 Bruce F. Molina, USGS

2007 Bruce F. Molina, USGS

Muir Inlet Glacier Glacier Bay National Park and Preserve, Alaska

1941 W. O. Field, # 41-64, National Snow and Ice Data Center and Glacier Bay National Park and Preserve Archive

1950 W. O. Field, #F50-R29, Glacier Bay National Park and Preserve Archive

2004 Bruce F. Molina, USGS

Thunderbird Glacier Glacier National Park, Montana

1907 Morton Elrod, GNP Archives

2007 Dan Fagre/Greg Pederson, USGS

A glacier's size can be easily measured.

Scientists know that most glaciers are melting. They think the melting is from a natural climate change speeded up by what humans do. Scientists will keep researching (studying) to learn more.

What could happen to rivers as glaciers melt and how could that affect the people who live downstream?

What could happen to the sea level as glaciers melt and how could that affect the people who live on islands or along the coasts?

How does the earth's climate affect a glacier?

Why are some glaciers and ice sheets melting and not others? So far, the Antarctic ice sheet is not melting, but the Arctic sheet in Greenland is.

How much freshwater might come out of melting glaciers?

Glaciers Around the World: True or False?

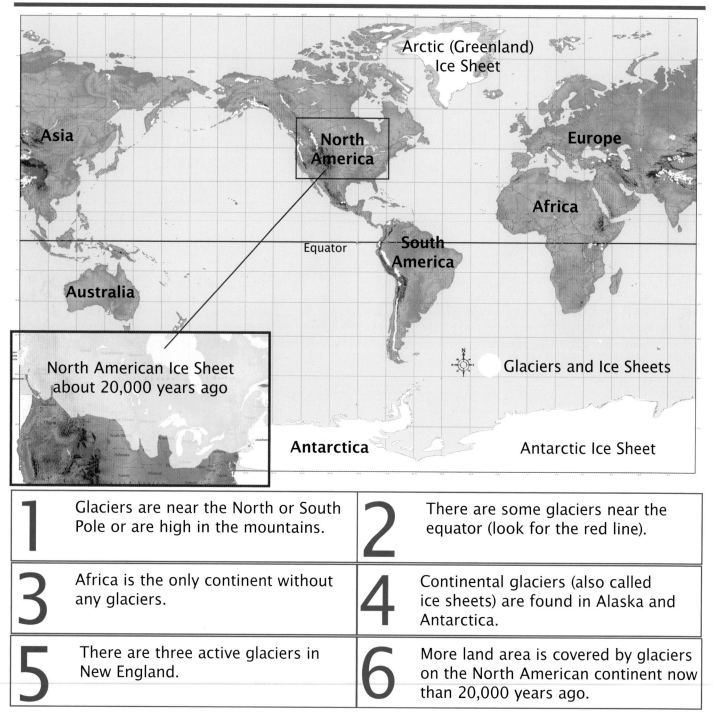

Arctic (Greenland) Ice Sheet

Asia

North America

Europe

Africa

Equator

South America

Australia

North American Ice Sheet about 20,000 years ago

N

Glaciers and Ice Sheets

Antarctica

Antarctic Ice Sheet

1	Glaciers are near the North or South Pole or are high in the mountains.	2	There are some glaciers near the equator (look for the red line).
3	Africa is the only continent without any glaciers.	4	Continental glaciers (also called ice sheets) are found in Alaska and Antarctica.
5	There are three active glaciers in New England.	6	More land area is covered by glaciers on the North American continent now than 20,000 years ago.

Answers: 1. True; 2. True: they are high in the mountains; 3. False: Africa does have glaciers but Australia does not; 4. False: there are only two ice sheets and they are found in Greenland and Antarctica; 5. False, there are signs of past glaciers in New England but the active glaciers in the US are in Alaska and in the western mountains; 6: False: an ice sheet covered much of the continent 20,000 years ago.

What Can We Do?

How can we help slow down the climate change?

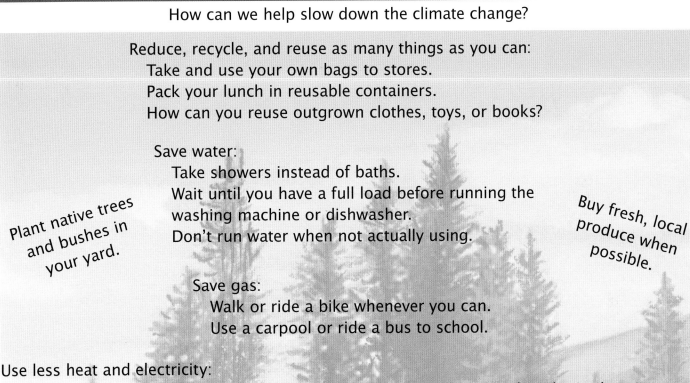

Reduce, recycle, and reuse as many things as you can:
Take and use your own bags to stores.
Pack your lunch in reusable containers.
How can you reuse outgrown clothes, toys, or books?

Save water:
Take showers instead of baths.
Wait until you have a full load before running the washing machine or dishwasher.
Don't run water when not actually using.

Plant native trees and bushes in your yard.

Buy fresh, local produce when possible.

Save gas:
Walk or ride a bike whenever you can.
Use a carpool or ride a bus to school.

Use less heat and electricity:
Keep house temperatures a few degrees warmer in the summer and cooler in the winter.
Adjust thermostats when you leave the house and at night.
Turn lights off when you leave a room.
Turn off TVs, computers, and other electrical equipment when you aren't using them.
Use energy-efficient light bulbs.

Water and Glaciers

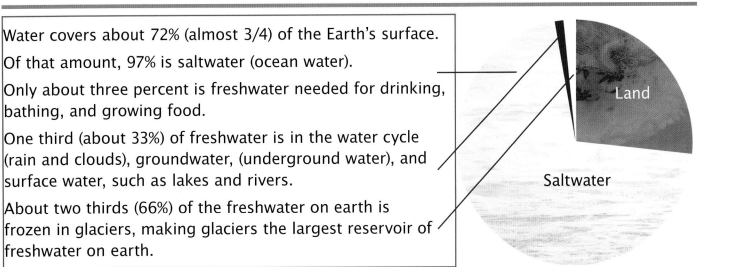

Water covers about 72% (almost 3/4) of the Earth's surface.

Of that amount, 97% is saltwater (ocean water).

Only about three percent is freshwater needed for drinking, bathing, and growing food.

One third (about 33%) of freshwater is in the water cycle (rain and clouds), groundwater, (underground water), and surface water, such as lakes and rivers.

About two thirds (66%) of the freshwater on earth is frozen in glaciers, making glaciers the largest reservoir of freshwater on earth.

Land

Saltwater

Animal Matching Activity

Match the animal to its description. Answers are upside down on the next page.

bighorn or
Dall sheep

ground squirrel

marmot

pika

snowshoe hare

white-tailed
ptarmigan

wolverine

1 These mammals easily climb up and down narrow cliffs on rocky mountaintops and feed on whatever plants and grass they find. The males (rams) have huge, curled horns that they use to fight each other for the females (ewes). These animals migrate down the mountain in the winter to where it is a little warmer and back up again for the summer.

2 These birds live in high mountain areas from Alaska to New Mexico. They can fly but prefer to walk and their feathered legs and toes keep them warm. Their feathers turn white during the winter to help hide in the snow but are a gray brown during the rest of the year. They eat berries and leaves from tundra plants. Some migrate down the mountain or small distances, following food in the winter.

3 There are several different types of these mammals adapted to a wide variety of habitats from hot deserts to cold mountaintops and the arctic. Some live in trees (maybe in your own backyard) and some live on the ground, like the one in this book. Most eat seeds and have a special "cheek pouch" to carry the seeds. They are related to chipmunks and most hibernate during the winter.

4 Because these mammals don't hibernate in winter when it can be hard to find food, these animals cut and dry plants during the summer and then save the plants in a "hay pile" in their burrows to eat during the winter.

5 These social mammals live in underground burrows and hibernate during the fall and winter. During the summer, while most are playing, one animal stands guard and will let the others know if danger approaches. These plant-eating animals will also eat snow to get the water they need.

6 Unlike their rabbit cousins, these plant-eating mammals are born with fur and able to see. Their fur turns white in the winter so they can "hide in plain sight." They even have fur on their long hind feet that help them to walk on top of the snow, like snowshoes. They have short ears that help them to stay warm in the winter.

7 These meat-eating mammals are shy but clever. They usually live alone and mark their territories with a strong smell. These animals have long guard hairs (on top of their fur) that trap air to help keep them warm and the snow and rain out. These fast-running animals kill prey with their very sharp teeth.

Alpine and Arctic Animal Adaptations

The animals in the book can be found in the same area (habitat) as you would find glaciers: high in the mountains (alpine) and the arctic. It gets very cold in the winter with a lot of snow and stays cold and windy during the summer. Animals living in these areas need to stay warm, hide in the snow and ice, and find or have food to eat (especially in the winter). Use the information and illustrations in the book and in the matching activity to answer the following questions. Answers are upside down, below.

1	Which animals have white fur or feathers in the winter to hide in the snow?	**2**	Which animals have fur or feathers on their feet?
3	Which animal gathers food during the summer to eat in the winter?	**4**	Which animals have little ears to stay warmer in the winter?
5	Which animal has big feet (like snowshoes) to walk on snow?	**6**	Which animals hibernate for the winter?
7	Which animals migrate for the winter?	**8**	Which animal is a bird?
9	Which animals are mammals?	**10**	Which animals eat plants (herbivores) and which eats meat (carnivore)?

Food for Thought

How is this story similar to and different than *The Sky is Falling*?

Why did Wiley Wolverine want the animals to go to his den? How did he try to trick them?

The animals in the story worry about what they will do and how they might live if the glaciers melt. What is each animal worried about?

Adaptation Answers: 1. ptarmigan, snowshoe hare; 2. ptarmigan, snowshoe hare; 3. pika; 4. pika, snowshoe hare; 5. snowshoe hare back feet; 6. marmot, some ground squirrels; 7. bighorn/Dall sheep, ptarmigan; 8. ptarmigan; 9. bighorn/Dall sheep, ground squirrel, pika, marmot, snowshoe hare, wolverine; 10. Herbivores: bighorn/Dall sheep, ptarmigan, ground squirrel, pika, marmot, snowshoe hare. Carnivore: wolverine

Matching Answers: 1. bighorn/Dall sheep, 2. white-tailed ptarmigan, 3. ground squirrel, 4. pika, 5. marmot, 6. snowshoe hare, 7. wolverine

For my first grandchild, Scarlet, with all my love—DL

In memory of my grandmothers, Ruth Zimmerman and Marie McNeil, with love—SB

Thanks to Doug Capra, Lead Interpretive Ranger, Exit Glacier, Kenai Fjords National Park for verifying the accuracy of the information in For Creative Minds.

Library of Congress Cataloging-in-Publication Data

Love, Donna, 1956-
  The glaciers are melting! / by Donna Love ; illustrated by Shennen Bersani.
    p. cm.
  ISBN 978-1-60718-126-2 (hardback) -- ISBN 978-1-60718-136-1 (pbk.) -- ISBN 978-1-60718-146-0 (English ebook) -- ISBN 978-1-60718-156-9 (Spanish ebook) 1. Glaciers--Juvenile literature. 2. Climatic changes--Environmental aspects--Juvenile literature. I. Bersani, Shennen, ill. II. Title.
  GB2403.8.L68 2011
  551.31'2--dc22

                    2010049638

Also available as eBooks featuring auto-flip, auto-read, 3D-page-curling, and selectable English and Spanish text and audio
Interest level: 004-009
Grade level: P-4
ATOS™ Level: 3.4
Lexile Level: 680 Lexile Code: AD
Curriculum keywords: adaptations, anthropomorphic, change environment, character: helping friends/animals, climate, compare/contrast, earth processes (fast/slow), EE (Environmental Education), geography, habitat, map, migration/hibernation, recycle, repeated lines

Manufactured in China, January, 2011
This product conforms to CPSIA 2008
First Printing
Sylvan Dell Publishing
612 Johnnie Dodds, Suite A2
Mt. Pleasant, SC 29464